3 3052 01323 3848

D0520416

HOOP HOTSHOT

BY JAKE MADDOX

illustrated by Sean Tiffany

text by Bob Temple

STONE ARCH BOOKS
www.stonearchbooks.com

Jake Maddox Books are published by Stone Arch Books,
A Capstone Imprint
1710 Roe Crest Drive
North Mankato, Minnesota 56003
www.capstonepub.com

Copyright © 2009 by Stone Arch Books

All rights reserved. No part of this publication may be reproduced
in whole or in part, or stored in a retrieval system, or transmitted in any
form or by any means, electronic, mechanical, photocopying, recording,
or otherwise, without written permission of the publisher.

Library of Congress Cataloging-in-Publication Data
Maddox, Jake.
    Hoop Hotshot / by Jake Maddox; illustrated by Sean Tiffany.
    p. cm. — (Impact Books. A Jake Maddox Sports Story)
    ISBN 978-1-4342-1202-3 (library binding)
    ISBN 978-1-4342-1400-3 (pbk.)
    [1. Basketball—Fiction. 2. Teamwork (Sports)—Fiction.]
I. Tiffany, Sean, ill. II. Title.
PZ7.M25643Hm 2009
[Fic]—dc22   2008031956

Summary:
Joe thinks of himself as "The Flash"—a hotshot basketball player
who knows the coolest moves. The other members of his team aren't as
impressed. Joe spends too much time trying to wow the crowd, and not
enough time helping the team. At tryouts for the freshman team, Joe is
quickly cut. He needs to stop fooling around and prove he has what it
takes to stay in the game.

Creative Director: Heather Kindseth
Graphic Designer: Carla Zetina-Yglesias

Printed in the United States of America in Stevens Point, Wisconsin.
072012
006847R

TABLE OF CONTENTS

CHAPTER 1

THE FLASH

Joe took a deep breath. He glanced down at his expensive basketball shoes.

Still shining, he thought. *Now it's time to turn up the heat.*

Joe looked up at the scoreboard. The game was tied, with one minute left.

This is my time, he thought.

From out of bounds, Joe's teammate passed the ball to him on one bounce.

Right away, Joe could tell there was a defender behind him. He had to move fast.

He faked left, then spun right, pounding the ball on the floor. *Whoosh*. He was past the first defender in a flash.

Joe sped up the court. Three teammates waited for a pass near the hoop, but Joe didn't care. All he saw was the bright orange rim.

As he crossed the half-court line, a defender ran over. Joe saw an open teammate out of the corner of his eye. Instead of passing the ball, Joe decided to take on the defender himself.

He dribbled right at the defender, almost too close. Then he quickly put the ball between his legs and moved left past the confused other player.

The lane was open for a second. But in the blink of an eye, two more defenders stepped into the lane.

Adam, one of his teammates and friends, was alone under the hoop. Joe could pass to him. But Joe's blood was pumping. He wanted to make the layup.

He faked his way past one of the defenders. Then Joe decided to challenge the last one. He leaped straight into the other player's path.

Joe was so close to the bucket. If he could shoot, he was sure he'd make it. He bumped into the defender's chest. Then Joe turned his body to the right, letting the ball roll off his fingertips up toward the rim.

Bleet! The official's whistle blew. Joe fell to the ground in a heap.

As he landed, he saw the ball drop through the net. He turned to the official. Just as he'd hoped, the official was pointing at the defender Joe had bumped into.

The crowd of parents and kids at courtside went crazy. "Way to go, Joe!" they called.

Joe hopped up and put his arms in the air. Some people cheered.

But not everyone was impressed. "There he goes again," Adam said to Brian, another one of Joe's teammates and friends. "He's always showing off."

Joe headed to the free throw line. He made the shot, bringing his team to a three-point lead. There was still plenty of time in the game, but Joe wasn't about to slow down.

On the next possession, Adam stole a pass. Joe moved away from the player he was guarding and broke down the court all alone. Adam passed him the ball.

Without a defender in sight, Joe could have easily just laid the ball up on the rim for the easy basket.

Instead, he drove hard to the hoop and jumped. He put the ball between his legs in midair before he finally reached up and put it in the hoop.

The crowd went nuts. They all cheered and clapped.

"That's why they call me The Flash!" Joe yelled.

Moments later, Brian grabbed a rebound. Joe sped out to the wing to catch the pass Brian threw him.

Joe brought the ball to the middle of the court. He had a teammate on each wing. One defender stepped in front of Joe to challenge him. Two teammates were wide open on the wings.

Everyone thought that Joe would keep the ball and go to the basket. Instead, he threw a behind-the-back pass to Adam, who was on his left.

The pass startled Adam, but he was able to catch it. He dribbled once and laid the ball in for a basket just before the final horn sounded.

In just one minute, Joe had helped his team score seven straight points for the victory.

Joe raised his arms in the air. "Oh, yeah!" he yelled. "The Flash strikes again!"

"We're both going to be hearing about this game for a long, long time," Adam whispered to Brian.

Brian rolled his eyes. He whispered back, "That's what we get for being best friends with The Flash."

[CHAPTER 2]

SMALL-TIME HERO

Joe, Adam, and Brian always walked home from games together. They headed out of the gym.

On his way out, Joe slapped hands with anyone who would give him five. Lots of people complimented Joe on his great play at the end of the game.

It took forever to get out of the gym. Once they were headed home, Joe started talking.

"Man, I was really The Flash today," he bragged. "Did you see how stupid I made that one kid look? He's probably still standing on that court, wondering what happened to him."

Adam and Brian glanced at each other. "Yeah, I saw that," Adam said. "I also saw the time you tried to pass the ball off the backboard to yourself, and lost it out of bounds."

"Yeah," Brian added, "and I saw the time you tried a fancy move on a kid and dribbled the ball off your foot out of bounds."

Joe laughed. "That's fine, that's fine, bring it on," he said. "We all know that without my plays at the end, we wouldn't have won."

"That's true, but if you would quit showing off the whole game, maybe we wouldn't need The Flash to save us at the end!" Adam said.

Joe shook his head. "Say what you want, but we haven't lost a game all year, have we?" he asked. Then he smiled. "I didn't think so."

The team's record was perfect. They had won every game all season.

But Adam and Brian knew that it wasn't all skill. They played in a community league. All of the teams were made up of kids who went to their school.

Adam, Joe, and Brian were three of the best players in the school, and they had all been put on the same team. Even before the season started, they were pretty sure that they'd win every game.

"No, we haven't lost — yet," Brian said. "But we're the best team in the league. We should be beating the other teams by twenty or thirty points every game. When you act like The Flash, we end up only winning by a few points at the end."

Adam nodded. "And one of these times, The Flash is going to fail," he added.

"No way, man," Joe said, shaking his head. "No way."

Adam said, "But what about next year?"

"What about next year?" Joe asked.

"Next year we all move up to the middle-school team," Brian explained. "All the kids on all the teams in our league will be trying out for one team next year. If you don't work on your real game, not the flashy one, you might not make it."

Joe laughed. "You've got to be kidding," he said. "Don't you guys know who you are talking to?"

"Yes, we know, we know," Adam said. He sighed. "We're talking to The Flash."

"That's right," Joe said.

Joe tried to forget about what his friends had said, but he couldn't.

At their school, there were eight teams in the league. Each team had ten players. The one team at the middle school only had room for fifteen players.

That meant that if all eighty guys from the community league tried out, sixty-five people wouldn't make it.

The Flash was trying hard to stop worrying.

[CHAPTER 3]

NEW TEAM

There were three games left in the season, and they were all the same. Brian, Adam, and Joe's team should have won all three games by a huge lead, but every time they started to pull ahead, Joe started acting like The Flash.

He would make risky passes, even when a better, simpler one was there for him. He would dribble behind his back or between his legs.

The people watching the game loved it, but The Flash didn't always do the right thing for his team.

Sometimes the ball would fly out of bounds, or the other team would steal it. The Flash was making it hard for his team to win.

Finally, in the closing minutes, Joe would win the game with a few flashy plays that worked. When he really needed to play well, he never failed.

At the end of the season, the team had a perfect record.

Joe wasn't worried anymore about whether he would make the middle-school basketball team. Any coach would see that he was the best!

* * *

The following October, it was time for tryouts at the middle school. Joe, Adam, and Brian felt ready. They had been playing basketball at the playground and in driveways since last season ended.

Adam was one of the tallest kids in the school. He was a very good rebounder, and he had some good moves near the basket to make shots. He always listened to his coaches, and he practiced even boring stuff, like dribbling.

Joe knew that Adam would make the team. He'd probably even be the starting center.

Joe was also pretty sure that Brian would make it. He was tall and usually made his shots. He also had a quick first step, so he could take the ball and beat his defender for a layup.

He was great on defense. Brian always worked hard on that end of the floor. He usually guarded the other team's best player.

Everybody knew that Joe was the most talented player in the school. Nobody could dribble the ball like him.

He could do more tricks than anyone else. Passes behind his back, dribbling through his legs, spin moves, double-pump shots — Joe could do it all.

More than fifty players from the boys' community league tried out for the middle-school team.

When the boys gathered for the first practice, Joe, Adam, and Brian looked around at the other players. Joe didn't feel nervous, but he was surprised by how many people were there.

"Man," Brian said. "It was one thing to play against these guys in the community league. Each team only had a few really good players."

"I know," Adam said. "Now all the good players are in the same room at the same time."

Joe shrugged. "I'm not worried," he said. "The Flash has tricks none of these guys have."

"Maybe the coach won't care that much about tricks," Adam said.

Joe laughed. "Yeah right!" he said. "Tricks are what the fans want!"

"All right, boys," the coach called out. "I'm Coach Jenkins. I have a really tough job. I have to pick fifteen of you to play on my team."

The coach smiled. Then he went on, "I'll tell you right now what I look for when I pick players. I look for talent, of course. But I also look for hard work, excellent defense, and rebounding. Most importantly, I look for players who will put the team ahead of themselves. So, here's our slogan for this year."

Coach Jenkins pulled a T-shirt out of his bag. On the front, it said, "Richmond Middle School Basketball." He turned it around. On the back was a drawing of a basketball. Underneath, it said: "We, Not Me."

[CHAPTER 4]

FLASH DRILLS

Adam and Brian looked at Joe. Joe just shook his head. "I'm not worried," he whispered.

Right away, Coach Jenkins ran the players through basic passing, defense, and rebounding drills.

Joe hated drills. He even hated the shooting drills, which most of the other kids loved. He just wanted to play ball. He wanted to show off his tricks.

"Man, this is boring," Joe said to Adam during a break in a drill. "When are we going to actually play some basketball?"

But they didn't play that day. At the practice the next day, they didn't play either. They just worked on drills.

Near the end of practice on the second day, Coach Jenkins blew his whistle. Everyone walked over to him.

"Trying to pick from this many players is hard," the coach said. "I decided to put you through a couple of days' worth of drills to see who has the basics down. We'll be cutting down to twenty players today. At the end of the week, I'll tell you who will be playing on the team."

Some of the guys started whispering. Coach Jenkins raised his hand for quiet.

"There will be a list in the locker room in ten minutes," he said. "If your name is on the list, then you are still on the team. If not, you should sign up for the community league so you can keep working on your skills."

After shooting for ten more minutes, Adam said, "I think it's been enough time."

"Let's go check out the list," Brian said. "Come on, Joe."

Joe laughed. "I'm not in a hurry," he said.

Adam and Brian looked at each other. "Okay," Adam said. Then he and Brian headed to the locker room. Joe followed, but he didn't look at the list. He just changed his clothes and got ready to go home.

Soon, Adam and Brian walked over. They started getting ready to leave.

"Why were you guys so worried?" Joe asked. "You knew you were going to be on the list."

"You can never be too sure," Adam replied, taking his gym bag out of his locker.

"Well, were you on the list?" Joe asked.

"Yes, I was," Adam said. "We all were."

"See what I mean?" Joe said. "Nothing to worry about."

[CHAPTER 5]

FLASHY MOVES

They finally played basketball the next day at practice. Joe was thrilled. They started with drills, but then it was time for a game of five-on-five.

As soon as the game started, Joe turned into The Flash. Right away, his teammates were frustrated. He almost never made a normal bounce pass. Instead, he'd throw a more difficult pass, sometimes without looking.

Once, the player he was passing to missed the catch because Joe's aim was off. Another time, the ball sailed right out of bounds.

When that happened, Coach Jenkins just shook his head. Adam noticed that the coach didn't seem pleased. His eyes lit up once when Joe faked out a defender and scored. But Coach Jenkins didn't seem very impressed with Joe's style.

Near the end of the game, Joe was leading a three-on-one fastbreak. A defender headed toward him, and Joe moved left.

When the defender moved the same way, the teammate on Joe's right was wide open. If Joe sent him an easy bounce pass, he could make the layup.

Instead, Joe leaped in the air and spun around fast. Then he tried to throw a behind-the-back pass to a different teammate. The defender reached out and easily blocked the pass. Another defender caught it, and within a few seconds, the opposing team had scored.

Bleeeeet! Coach Jenkins' whistle blew. "That's it!" he yelled. "We're done for today. Hit the showers." Then he added, "Joe, please stay here for a minute."

Joe proudly walked over to the coach. He was sure that Coach Jenkins would tell him what a great player he was.

"Joe, I think you are one of the most talented players out here," the coach said. "You might be the most talented. But you're throwing it away, just like you threw away that pass."

Joe felt confused. "What?" he asked.

"There have been a lot of players with fancy moves," Coach Jenkins said. "Some of the greatest players ever had some really fancy moves. But what made them great was that they knew the right time to use them.

"If you know great moves, the right time to use them is all the time!" Joe said, smiling.

Coach Jenkins frowned. "A flashy play is also a risky play," he said. "On that last play, you had a wide-open teammate. That would've been an easy pass. Whenever you can, make the easy pass. Save the flashy ones for when it's your only option. Then, the flashy play will also be the smart play. Get it?"

"But Coach, they call me The Flash," Joe said. "That's who I am. That's how I play."

"No, Joe," the coach said. "You call yourself The Flash. Nicknames like that have to be earned."

Joe looked down at the ground.

"I think you can be a great player," Coach Jenkins said. "But if you want to play on my team, you have to learn when to make those flashy plays. You also have to know when to play it safe. Remember, it's about the team. We, not me."

"Got it, Coach," Joe replied. "We, not me."

[CHAPTER 6]

A TOUGH LESSON

Joe stormed into the locker room. He couldn't believe what Coach Jenkins had just said.

Was he saying that if Joe didn't change his playing style, he would sit on the bench? Or worse, was the coach saying that The Flash might get cut?

"No way," Joe whispered. "No way." He quickly changed his clothes. Then he, Adam, and Brian headed home.

When they were away from the school building, Adam asked, "What did Coach Jenkins want to talk to you about?"

"You wouldn't believe me if I told you," Joe replied.

"Come on," Brian said.

"He actually told me that I needed to play boring in order to make the team," Joe said.

"That's exactly what he said?" Adam asked, looking at Joe. "He told you to play boring?"

"Well, not exactly," Joe said. "He said something about knowing when to play safe and when to be flashy. He said everything I did needed to help the team. You know, 'We, not me.' That means play boring!"

"I don't know. It sounds like good advice to me," Brian said.

"Oh yeah?" Joe said. Frowning, he turned to face his friend. "Well, I have my own version of 'We, not me.' It goes like this: *We* do not win without *me*."

"Nice," Adam said, shaking his head. "Before you put that on a shirt, you might want to think about what the coach said."

"I did think about it," Joe said. "I've decided it's stupid." He sighed. Then he said, "See you guys tomorrow. I'm going this way." He quickly turned onto a different street.

"Should we follow him?" Brian asked.

Adam shook his head. "Nah," he said. "He'll change his mind by tomorrow. He just has to cool off."

* * *

At practice the next afternoon, Joe was worse than ever. He launched shots even when a defender was right in front of him.

He threw passes behind his back, without looking, and while he was spinning in the air.

He drove to the basket when he should have passed. He shot three-pointers when there was an open teammate waiting under the basket.

Some of his crazy plays worked. At one point, he stole the ball and broke to the basket alone.

Instead of taking the easy layup, he tossed the ball around his waist to his other hand. Then he quickly laid the ball in left-handed.

The ball fell through the hoop, and Joe yelled, "Wooo hooo! The Flash is back!"

No one else cheered.

Coach Jenkins's face turned red. "Hit the showers, Joe," he said quietly. "You're done for today. If you can't play smart basketball, you won't play at all."

Shocked, Joe stood silently in front of the nineteen other players. They all stared at him, but no one spoke.

Joe opened his mouth, but no words came out. He looked at Adam and Brian, but they both quickly looked down at the ground.

Joe stood there, all alone. Then he turned and ran into the locker room.

[CHAPTER 7]

CUT

The next day was the last day of tryouts. For the first time, Joe was worried about his place on the team.

He knew the coach was angry at him. But was Coach Jenkins angry enough to actually cut The Flash?

Practice was hard that day. The team did a lot of running and drills. They played full-court five-on-five for only few minutes.

Joe did his best to play smart. He tried to focus on his team. But it didn't seem to work. Joe was so used to being The Flash that he couldn't remember how to be a good teammate. He didn't know how to communicate.

At the end of practice, Coach Jenkins called the players to mid-court. "Making these cuts was really hard," he said. "There are a lot of great players here. But I could only choose ten players for the team. So, in ten minutes, I'll post a list down in the locker room. If your name is on the list, you made the team. Thank you all for your hard work!"

Joe wanted to see the list right away this time. He headed to the locker room and changed quickly. Then he rushed to the coach's office to see the list.

Joe was the first one to look at the list. He quickly read the names. Adam was at the top. Brian was also on the list.

Joe's name wasn't there.

Coach Jenkins walked out of the office. He stood next to Joe.

"Let's go in my office and talk," the coach said quietly.

Joe didn't say anything. He slowly stepped into the coach's office.

"Joe, do you know why your name isn't on the list?" the coach asked.

"I guess so," Joe replied. "I didn't play smart enough, right?"

"That's right," the coach replied. "You have a lot of talent, but you need to learn how to use it."

The coach pulled open one of his desk drawers and reached in. He pulled out a DVD and handed it to Joe. It wasn't a DVD with a fancy case and label. It was homemade, and the label was in someone's handwriting.

Joe slowly read the title out loud. "Basketball's Greatest Playmakers," he said. "What's this?"

Coach Jenkins smiled. "I was a point guard too," he told Joe. "This DVD has some of the greatest point guards in the history of basketball on it. There are some guys who play today and some old-school guys. But this isn't like a regular sports video. This isn't all of their greatest plays. This DVD shows highlights of them making great plays look easy."

"Huh?" Joe said.

"Anyone can make an easy play look hard," the coach said. "You just add a little flash. But a real superstar makes hard plays look easy."

"Well, thanks, I guess," Joe said.

"Don't forget to sign up for the community league," Coach Jenkins said.

"Okay. I guess I will," Joe said. Then he turned to leave the coach's office. He held the DVD in one hand and his basketball shoes in the other. He wasn't looking forward to what lay ahead — another year in the community league.

CHAPTER 8

COMMUNITY LEAGUE

When Joe showed up for the first practice with his community league team, he wanted things to be different. He wanted to do what Coach Jenkins had said. But his new teammates wanted to see The Flash.

"Hey, Joe's on our team!" one of them shouted when Joe walked into the gym.

"Awesome!" another kid said. "We're definitely going to win the championship!"

Joe smiled, but he wasn't thinking about being The Flash. He had spent hours watching Coach Jenkins's DVD. He thought he had learned a few things. He wanted to try to play the game differently. He wanted to start playing smart.

A few weeks later, Joe's team played their first game. When Joe didn't show off his awesome plays, his teammates were surprised.

At first, Joe wasn't very good. He was used to being The Flash. It turned out that without The Flash's moves, Joe didn't have the skill he thought he did.

Joe wanted to try to thrill everyone in the gym, but he held back. He walked the ball up the court as he dribbled, instead of running.

He carefully set up the team's plays, instead of just thinking about his own. He made obvious passes, not risky ones.

But because Joe was being so careful, the defense figured out what his plans were. They knew who Joe was passing the ball to every time he made a pass, and lots of his passes were stolen.

The other team figured out his plans. They would run up and dribbled his ball away. They almost always could tell what play he was planning. With each bad play, Joe felt worse. His team lost. And they kept losing, game after game.

Joe really wanted to show off The Flash again.

One Saturday morning, Adam and Brian came to watch Joe's game. It was another awful game.

Joe wasn't showing off. In fact, it seemed like he was afraid to ever take a risk — even when a risky play was the right thing to do.

His team fell further and further behind. Joe felt worse and worse.

Joe's coach and teammates were mad too. Finally, during a timeout, one of Joe's teammates ran over to him.

"What is wrong with you?" the guy yelled. "Why aren't you trying?"

Joe just looked at the ground. He didn't know what to say. But he knew one thing. He couldn't hold back any longer. He was hurting his team too much.

Joe's team trailed by six points, with thirty seconds to play. Finally, the ball reached Joe's hands.

He bolted for the other end of the court. His stunned teammates stood still and let him go.

Joe sped through the defense. He pulled free from the last defender. Then he made a basket.

As soon as the ball was in play again, Joe stole it back. A defender charged at him, but Joe dribbled between his legs to get free. Then he soared under the basket for a layup.

Suddenly, Joe's team trailed by just two points.

The other team's point guard tried to pass the ball up court, but Joe got a finger on it. The ball headed for the sideline. Joe ran for it. As he did, he saw one of his teammates, Paul, rushing down the court.

Joe grabbed the ball and tossed a no-look, over-the-shoulder pass to Paul. Paul caught the ball and laid it in, just as he was fouled.

The fans cheered. They cheered again when Paul made the free throw to clinch the victory. Joe ran over to Paul. He smacked him on the back and shouted, "Way to go!"

As the noise died down, Joe saw a face he knew standing with the other fans. There, next to Adam and Brian, was Coach Jenkins.

[CHAPTER 9]

Coach Jenkins, Adam, and Brian stared at Joe.

Suddenly, Joe didn't feel much like celebrating anymore. He knew he had just unleashed The Flash in front of Coach Jenkins. And Coach Jenkins didn't like The Flash.

Joe walked over to the sideline. "Hey guys," he said to his friends.

Then, nervously, he looked at Coach Jenkins. "Hey, Coach," he said quietly.

"Hi, Joe," the coach said. "Nice win."

"Um, thanks," Joe replied. "I guess it got a little crazy at the end. But I'm not The Flash anymore. Really. I mean, in the beginning of the game it was nothing like that."

Coach Jenkins nodded. "I saw the whole game, Joe," the coach said. "You don't need to tell me what happened."

"Oh," Joe said. "Well, I'm working on it. I swear. I'm trying to figure out how to be good and play smart." He looked down at his shoes.

"I can tell," the coach said. "It looked to me like at the end there, you figured it out."

Joe looked at Coach Jenkins. "What do you mean?" he asked.

"The last thirty seconds of that game is exactly how I wanted you to play," Coach Jenkins said, smiling. "For example, on the first basket, you used your speed and a great spin move to get an easy basket. Then you played hard defense and got the ball back."

"Yeah, I guess so," Joe said.

"On the second one, you put the ball between your legs, but that was the only move you could make to get away from the defender," the coach went on. "You didn't do it to show off. You did it to make a play."

Joe smiled. "Yeah, I guess you're right," he said.

"Then you worked hard to get the ball back and made a great pass to an open teammate, and let him get the tying and winning points," the coach said. "And you made it all look easy."

Joe blushed. "Thanks, Coach," he said. "Hey, why did you come to the game?"

"I came to see how you were doing," the coach said. "You see, our regular point guard is moving out of town, so there's a spot open on the middle-school team. I wanted to see if you had learned anything."

Coach Jenkins paused. Joe felt like the pause lasted forever. He stared down at his shoes again, waiting.

Finally, the coach patted him on the back. "And I think you have," he said.

"Thanks," Joe said.

"In fact, if you can take that last thirty seconds and play like that all the time, I think we may have a spot for you on the middle-school team," the coach finished, smiling.

"Yeah!" Joe shouted. "The Flash is back!"

Coach Jenkins's smile quickly turned into a frown.

Joe laughed. "Just kidding, Coach," he said. "Just kidding."

* * *

After school the next day, Joe practiced with the Richmond Middle School team. Just a week later, he was in the starting lineup when the team played its next game.

Very early in Joe's first middle-school game, the other team missed a shot. Adam pulled down the rebound and quickly passed the ball to Joe. He and Brian ran up the court.

Joe pushed the ball up the left side of the court. He gave a head fake that drew the defender closer to him, leaving Brian all alone.

Seeing the opening, Joe dropped a simple bounce pass. It went straight to Brian's hands. Then Brian made an easy layup.

As the ball dropped through the hoop, all of the fans, parents, and Joe's teammates cheered.

"Great pass, Joe!" Coach Jenkins called. "Smart play!"

For the rest of the game, Joe made play after play, setting up teammates for open shots, hustling on defense, and using his speed to score easy baskets.

When the game reached the final minute, Joe's team led by fifteen points. The Flash didn't need to save the day this time. Joe had already done it.

ABOUT THE AUTHOR

Bob Temple lives in Rosemount, Minnesota, with his wife and three children. He has written more than thirty books for children. Over the years, he has coached more than twenty kids' soccer, basketball, and baseball teams. He also loves visiting classrooms to talk about his writing.

ABOUT THE ILLUSTRATOR

When Sean Tiffany was growing up, he lived on a small island off the coast of Maine. Every day, from sixth grade until he graduated from high school, he had to take a boat to get to school. When Sean isn't working on his art, he works on a multimedia project called "OilCan Drive," which combines music and art. He has a pet cactus named Jim.

GLOSSARY

challenge (CHAL-uhnj)—invite someone to fight or try to do something

communicate (kuh-MYOO-nuh-kate)—share information with someone else

community (kuh-MYOO-nuh-tee)—people from the same area live in the same community

compliment (KOM-pluh-ment)—to tell someone that they have done a good job

confused (kuhn-FYOOZD)—if someone doesn't understand something, they are confused

defender (di-FEN-dur)—a player trying to stop points from being scored by the other team

league (LEEG)—a group of teams

official (uh-FISH-uhl)—a person who enforces the rules

possession (puh-ZESH-uhn)—if your team has possession, it has the ball

risky (RISK-ee)—dangerous

slogan (SLOH-guhn)—a phrase used by a group to express a belief

MORE ABOUT THE HARLEM GLOBETROTTERS

Flips, spins, and other crazy antics are common sights at a Harlem Globetrotters game.

The Harlem Globetrotters started as a serious basketball team. Then their tricks and funny routines became famous. The team began to focus more on entertaining the crowd than on playing serious basketball.

At every game, you will see players juggling multiple basketballs and spinning balls on their fingertips. The Globetrotters do crazy things, like make passes between their opponents' legs. They make difficult shots look easy.

The Globetrotters even helped invent the slam dunk, which is now part of every NBA game.

Many famous basketball players have played with the Globetrotters. Wilt Chamberlain, John Chaney, and Nat Clifton were all members of the team.

The Harlem Globetrotters travel around the world to take on their opponents. Even with their famous focus on tricks and entertainment, they rarely lose a game. At one time, they won 8,829 games in a row! And more importantly, they have fun on the court.

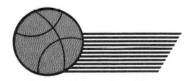

DISCUSSION QUESTIONS

1. Why didn't Coach Jenkins and the other players like it when Joe acted like The Flash?

2. What are some ways to handle it when someone is hogging the spotlight and not being a good teammate, like Joe does in this book?

3. At the end of this book, Joe has stopped being The Flash. Do you think he'll go back to his old ways? Why or why not?

WRITING PROMPTS

1. Have you ever been friends with or played on a team with someone like The Flash? What did you do to make sure he or she started to show better teamwork?

2. Joe got cut from the middle-school team. What do you think would have happened if he'd made the team? Write about it.

3. Joe liked to call himself The Flash. Think up a new nickname for yourself. What is it? Explain why you've given yourself that name.

JAKE MADDOX

GRIDIRON BULLY

SPORTS FICTION

Juan can't catch, he can't throw, and one of the members of the team hasn't been making it easy for Juan to feel at home on the football team. Can the ex-track star learn his new sport in time for the biggest game of the season?

BY JAKE MADDOX

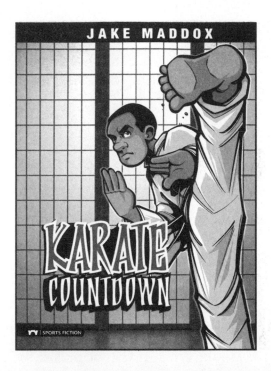

When Kenny's anger problem gets out of control, his father signs him up for karate lessons. But even in karate class, Kenny can't get a grip on his temper. With help from his karate teacher, will Kenny be able to calm down long enough to focus — and win?

INTERNET SITES

Do you want to know more about subjects related to this book? Or are you interested in learning about other topics? Then check out FactHound, a fun, easy way to find Internet sites.

Our investigative staff has already sniffed out great sites for you!

Here's how to use FactHound:

1. Visit *www.facthound.com*

2. Select your grade level.

3. To learn more about subjects related to this book, type in the book's ISBN number: **9781434212023**.

4. Click the **Fetch It** button.

FactHound will fetch the best Internet sites for you!